Pip the Prize Kitten

"Maybe John thinks *I'll* win a prize when we all go to the cat show next week," Pip mewed.

Lucinda and Angelica looked at each other in that snooty way they had.

"What do you mean?" Angelica spat. "*You* won't be going to the cat show!"

"You're not a *pedigree* cat!" Lucinda hissed. "You can't win a prize!"

Titles in Jenny Dale's KITTEN TALES™ series

More of Jenny Dale's KITTEN TALES™ stories
follow soon!

All of Jenny Dale's KITTEN TALES books can
be ordered at your local bookshop or are
available by post from Book Service by Post
(tel: 01624 675137)

Pip the Prize Kitten

by Jenny Dale

Illustrated by Susan Hellard

A Working Partners Book

MACMILLAN CHILDREN'S BOOKS

To Lily and Daisy

Special thanks to Narinder Dhami

First published 2001 by Macmillan Children's Books
a division of Macmillan Publishers Limited
25 Eccleston Place, London SW1W 9NF
Basingstoke and Oxford
www.macmillan.com

Associated companies throughout the world

Created by Working Partners Limited
London W6 0QT

ISBN 0 330 39735 4

3 5 7 9 8 6 4 2

A CIP catalogue record for this book is available from
the British Library.

Typeset by SX Composing DTP, Rayleigh, Essex
Printed and bound in Great Britain by Mackays of Chatham plc, Kent

Chapter One

"Say goodbye to Emily, Pip," said Pip's new owner, John Walker. "She's going to miss you." John held Pip's cat basket up, so that the kitten could see out of the car window.

"Bye, Emily," Pip mewed, as John's mum drove off down the

road. Emily, who was in John's class at school, stood at her gate, waving.

"Don't worry, Pip," said John, as he settled the basket on his knees again. He pushed his fingers through the wire door, and scratched Pip's fluffy little head. "Emily will come and visit you."

"Pip's a bit bigger than I thought she'd be," Mrs Walker said, braking to a halt at the traffic lights. "How old did you say she was?"

"She's fourteen weeks," said John. "The family who were going to have Pip changed their minds, so Emily had to find a new owner. That's why she put an advert up on the school

6

noticeboard."

Pip began to purr. She'd watched Emily making that notice, and had wondered who her new owner was going to be. All her brothers and sisters had already gone to their new homes weeks ago, and Pip had started to get a bit worried. Then John had seen the advert, and had come to Emily's to meet Pip. The kitten had liked him straight away.

"She's a lovely little thing," Mrs Walker said. "Although, you know, you *could* have had a pedigree kitten, John. I did offer to buy you one."

Pip's ears perked up, and her big, amber eyes blinked. She'd never heard of such a thing. "A *pedigree* kitten?" she miaowed. "What's that?"

Maybe pedigree kittens were different, Pip thought. Maybe they had six legs. Or two tails. Or maybe they were a special colour – green or pink. Or even purple, Pip decided. Pip's own coat was the same as her mum's – a bit mixed up, really – brown, black, orange, white . . . But she quite liked it.

"I didn't *want* a pedigree kitten, Mum," John said firmly. "The two we have already are enough!"

Pip's ears pricked up. "You mean, you've got two other cats for me to play with?" she purred, rubbing her head against John's hand. "Brilliant!"

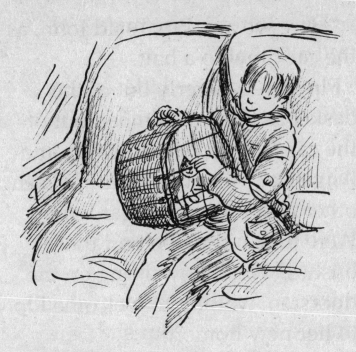

Mrs Walker laughed. "Yes, pedigree cats *do* need a lot of looking after," she agreed. "I wonder how Lucinda and Angelica will get on with Pip?"

Pip didn't care if Lucinda and Angelica were pedigree cats or not. She couldn't wait to get to her new home!

"Here we are, Pip," said John, as the car drew to a halt.

Pip stared eagerly out of the basket as they all climbed out of the car. Where were Lucinda and Angelica? Were they chasing each other round the front garden? Were they hiding behind those bushes? Were they sitting on the doorstep, waiting to welcome Pip to her new home?

But Pip couldn't see the other cats anywhere.

As John carried her into the house, Pip sniffed the air, her whiskers twitching. There were lots of new smells to get used to. But the two most interesting were cat smells. Lucinda and Angelica! But where were they?

"Out you come, Pip." John put the cat basket down on the living room floor and opened its door.

Pip stepped out, her eyes wide. She couldn't help feeling just a little nervous.

Suddenly the living room door swung open. Pip stared as two cats stepped into the room side by side, the tips of their tails waving.

They were the two most beautiful cats that Pip had ever seen. One was snowy white all over, and her coat was long and fluffy. She had large, round, blue eyes. The other cat had a smooth, silvery coat and slanting golden eyes. They both stared haughtily at Pip.

"Hello, I'm Lucinda Snowqueen Whitepaws," the white cat mewed, her pink nose in the air. "I'm a Persian."

"Hello, I'm Angelica Spring Blossom," mewed the other cat, arching her back. "And I'm a Lilac Burmese."

"Er – hello, I'm Pip," Pip replied

nervously. "And I'm a . . . kitten."

Lucinda and Angelica looked at each other.

Lucinda swayed over to twine herself around Mrs Walker's ankles. "You can't be a *pedigree* kitten with a plain name like that," she purred.

"And you're *definitely* not a competition cat, are you?" Angelica yawned. She sat down to wash her face with an elegant silver paw.

Pip brightened up a bit. "Yes, I am!" she miaowed back. "I used to have lots of competitions with my brothers and sisters – who could run the fastest, and whose claws were the sharpest, and—"

"Don't be silly!" Lucinda hissed

sharply. "What Angelica means is that you don't go to cat shows, like we do."

"What's a cat show?" Pip mewed, puzzled.

But both cats turned their backs on Pip and stalked out of the living room without answering.

Pip felt very small and sad as she watched them go. Lucinda and Angelica didn't think much of her at all.

"Come on, Pip." John scooped his kitten up and gave her a cuddle. "Let's get you something to eat," he said, and carried her into the kitchen.

Pip snuggled herself under her new owner's chin and purred in relief. At least John liked her.

Chapter Two

For the first few days in her new home, Pip had great fun playing with John. Lucinda and Angelica were still being unfriendly, but Pip didn't care too much. Then John went back to school. And Mrs Walker went to work. Pip felt a bit lonely and bored on her own.

In the back garden, she looked up at a blackbird sitting in the branches of a tree. "Will *you* come and play with me?" Pip mewed. "I promise I won't eat you."

But the blackbird ruffled up its feathers, and flew off. "Not likely!" it called.

Pip slowly sharpened her claws on the tree trunk. "I haven't got *anyone* to play with," she mewed miserably. "Maybe I should try a bit harder to make friends with Lucinda and Angelica."

Cheering up a bit, Pip padded back across the lawn to the cat flap in the kitchen door. She peeped through and saw Angelica sitting on the worktop, her tail swinging to and fro.

Lucinda was finishing off Pip's breakfast.

What a cheek! Pip thought to herself. But she decided not to make a fuss. As she pushed open the cat flap to climb inside, she could hear what the other cats were saying.

"Yes, I think I'm going to do very well at next week's show,"

Angelica purred. "I'm almost sure to come first in the Burmese class." She sounded very proud of herself. "In fact," she added, "I might even win Best Cat in the Whole Show."

Lucinda delicately swallowed the last bit of Pip's chicken-flavoured *Purrfect Chunks*. "Oh, really, Angelica!" she miaowed. "It's much more likely that *I* will win the Best in Show prize."

"Hello," Pip mewed, as she stepped into the kitchen. "Do you want to play?"

Lucinda and Angelica stared at the kitten. "*Play*?" they both miaowed haughtily. "Who with?"

"With me!" Pip mewed.

"*You?*" The cats stared even harder.

Pip sat down and sighed. Maybe this wasn't such a good idea, after all. "Yes," she mewed back. "We could chase each other round the garden. Or catch leaves."

"Oh, we don't do that sort of thing," Angelica sniffed.

"Goodness me, no, we don't!" agreed Lucinda. "Imagine having to brush leaves and twigs out of my fluffy coat!" She shuddered at the thought.

"Oh . . ." Pip mewed, feeling disappointed. "Well, we could play games here, in the house."

"Like what?" Angelica leaped down lightly from the worktop.

"Well, chasing each other up and down the stairs." Pip thought back to the games she'd played with her brothers and sisters. "Or hiding under the beds. Or climbing up the curtains. Or—"

"We haven't got time to play silly games like that." Lucinda yawned. "We need our beauty sleep." She began to curl up in her basket, ready for a nap.

"Yes, we *must* look our best for the cat show next week." Angelica sat down, and began to clean the silky fur around her face.

"Tell me about the cat show," Pip mewed eagerly. She still didn't know what a cat show was. And maybe Lucinda and

Angelica would be more friendly if she asked them about something *they* were interested in.

"What do *you* want to know about the cat show for?" Lucinda sniffed. But sure enough, she sat up again, wide awake. And Angelica stopped washing her face too. Pip could see that the two cats couldn't *wait* to tell her all about it.

"As you know, Lucinda and I are competition cats," Angelica began snootily. "Mrs Walker takes us to cat shows. Lots of pedigree cat owners take their cats there."

"Some other people at the shows, called judges, decide which cats are the best," Lucinda went on. "And the best cats win prizes."

"Oh!" Pip's amber eyes were round with wonder. Cat shows sounded like *great* fun. "So what do you have to do to win a prize? Do you have to show how fast you can run, and how high you can jump?"

Lucinda and Angelica blinked crossly at Pip.

"Of course not," Angelica hissed. "It's all about how beautiful you look."

"Oh." Pip thought about that. "Have you or Lucinda ever won a prize?" she mewed.

Both cats suddenly looked rather embarrassed. Lucinda pretended to clean her tail, and Angelica stared at the cat flap, as

if something outside had caught her attention.

"Well, have you?" Pip asked.

"Not yet," Lucinda mewed reluctantly. "Anyway, Mrs Walker has only just started taking us to shows. We're bound to win a prize soon!"

"That's why we need to keep ourselves clean and beautiful." Angelica gave Pip a snooty stare. "And that's why Mrs Walker brushes us every day, and gives us special food."

Pip looked at her empty food dish. She thought of the ordinary chicken-flavoured *Purrfect Chunks* that Lucinda had finished off when she thought no one was looking. Pip thought that was rather funny. But she didn't want to offend Lucinda, so she didn't mention it.

Instead, she mewed, "Maybe John thinks *I'll* win a prize when we all go to the cat show next week." She couldn't wait. It would be really exciting.

Lucinda and Angelica looked at each other in that snooty way they had.

"What do you mean?" Angelica spat. "*You* won't be going to the cat show!"

"You're not a *pedigree* cat!" Lucinda hissed. "You can't win a prize!"

Chapter Three

"I'm going to lie in my cage like *this*." Lucinda purred. She arranged herself on the sofa cushions in an elegant pose, her long, thick tail curled neatly around her. "And then when the judge comes along, I'm going to stand up like *this*." She climbed neatly to her feet, and stood with her nose and her tail in the air.

"And I'm going to purr like this, all the time the judge is looking at me," purred Angelica loudly.

"I'm going to lie quietly in the judges' arms when they pick me up," Lucinda added, trying to purr louder than Angelica. "They don't like it if you move around too much."

"*And* they like you to look interested," Angelica miaowed, giving Lucinda a cross look. Then she accidentally-on-purpose stepped on the other cat's paw. "They want to see what a nice personality you've got!"

"Well, *I'll* be all right then, won't I!" Lucinda hissed,

head-butting Angelica's bottom in return.

"Ooh!" Angelica sat down and glared at Lucinda. "I'm nicer than you are!"

"No, you're not!" Lucinda spat.

"Here we go again!" Pip mewed to herself. It was the day of the cat show, and she was curled up on the armchair, watching Lucinda and Angelica do their last-minute practice. Actually, Pip really wanted to have a nap, but Lucinda and Angelica were making so much noise with their purring and squabbling, she couldn't get any sleep at all.

It had been the same for the whole of the last week. Lucinda and Angelica were so nervous about the cat show coming up, they'd hissed and spat at Pip whenever she went near them.

The two cats had washed themselves every day for hours at a time. They had practised walking up and down as if they were supermodels. They had tried out different kinds of purrs. They made sure that Mrs Walker brushed them every day. John's mum had even given both cats a bath. Pip hadn't liked the look of *that*.

And now that the great day had come, Lucinda and Angelica were even *more* nervous. Pip couldn't help feeling a bit sorry for them.

"I think I'll wave my tail like *this*." Angelica began to swish her tail from side to side, and accidentally smacked Lucinda across the face.

"Ouch!" Lucinda was furious. "You did that on purpose, Angelica!" And she nipped the other cat's tail spitefully.

"Ow!" Angelica's golden eyes lit up with fury, and she flexed her razor-sharp claws. "I'm going to

pull your fur out for that, Lucinda!"

"No, I'm going to pull *your* fur out!" Lucinda hissed angrily.

"Stop it!" Pip jumped down from the armchair. "The judges won't be very impressed if you're both bald!"

Lucinda and Angelica glared at Pip.

"I suppose she's right," Angelica mewed reluctantly.

"Even if she *doesn't* know anything about cat shows," Lucinda agreed snootily.

Pip didn't say anything. But after hearing Lucinda and Angelica go on about cat shows all week, Pip felt as if she knew *everything* about them!

She knew that you had to be brave, and not be scared by all the other people and their cats. She knew that you had to be good when the judge picked you up, and purr happily, and not scratch or struggle or bite. Oh, yes, Pip knew all about it.

But I'm *not even* going *to the cat show*, Pip thought sadly. In fact, she was going to be left all alone for the first time ever, because John was going to the show too.

Oh, well, Pip thought, trying to cheer herself up, *at least I'll be able to have a nap in peace!*

Just then John and Mrs Walker came in, carrying some brushes and combs.

"Come on, girls," John's mum

said with a smile. "Time for your final grooming!"

"Me first!" Lucinda miaowed loudly, rushing across the room.

"No, me first!" Angelica leaped forward, stepping on Lucinda's tail and making her howl.

"Come on, Pip." John lifted his kitten on to his lap and began to brush her. "We've got to make sure you look your best too!"

"Why should Pip look her best?" Angelica mewed, arching her back as John's mum brushed her. "*She's* not coming to the cat show!"

"No, she's too ordinary," Lucinda added unkindly.

Pip was puzzled too. She patted her owner on the arm. "Why *are*

you brushing me, John?" she
purred.

John tickled his kitten's furry
tummy. "Maybe Pip will win a
prize, Mum," he said with a grin.

Pip's eyes opened wide. She
stared up at John. "You mean, I'm
going to the cat show too?"

Chapter Four

"This is ridiculous!" Lucinda mewed furiously, glaring at Pip. "How can *she* be going to the cat show? She's not even a pedigree cat!"

"I know," Angelica agreed. "I'm going to complain to the judges! It shouldn't be allowed."

Pip crept further towards the back of her basket, and tried to hide under her blanket. They were all in the car on their way to the cat show. At first, Pip had been really thrilled to hear that she was taking part. But now she was starting to feel worried. How could an ordinary pet kitten like her compete with beautiful, pedigree cats like Lucinda and Angelica?

"Everyone at the show's going to laugh at you," Angelica miaowed snootily.

"Yes, they're going to wonder what on earth you're doing there," Lucinda added haughtily.

Pip felt very miserable. Lucinda and Angelica must be right.

Just then John turned round in his seat to smile at her. "Are you OK, Pip?" he asked. "Not very far to go now."

Pip felt a bit better. There *was* someone who thought she was special – John! And if John thought she was good enough to go to the cat show, then maybe she was, whatever Angelica and Lucinda said.

"So which class will Pip be in?" Angelica mewed scornfully. "How about the *Most Mixed-up Coat* class?"

"Or the *Most Miserable Moggy* class?" Lucinda yawned.

Pip tried not to take any notice. Lucinda and Angelica might be beautiful on the outside, but they weren't very nice *inside*, she thought.

"What's the matter with Lucinda and Angelica?" John twisted round in his seat again to stare at the two pedigree cats. "They look really grumpy. If they're not careful, they'll frighten the judges!"

"Well!" Angelica sniffed, looking outraged.

"I've never been so insulted!" Lucinda hissed, and both cats turned their backs in a huff.

Pip began to purr a little. That had shown *them*! She decided that whatever happened, she was going to enjoy the cat show and do her best.

*

But when John carried Pip into the show, she began to feel scared all over again.

The show was being held in a large hall. Pip had never seen so many people – or so many cats! There were hundreds and hundreds of them, lined up in cages, all waiting for the judges to look at them.

Pip's eyes widened in surprise as she spotted a whole row of snowy white cats like Lucinda. And then a row of elegant silvery cats like Angelica. Pip had thought that Lucinda and Angelica were the only white and silver cats in the whole world!

"Right, first we have to take the cats to be checked over by the

vet," said Mrs Walker, who had
Angelica's basket in one hand
and Lucinda's in the other.

"Don't be scared, Pip," John
said softly, as they joined the
queue of cat owners at the vet's
table. "It's just to make sure that
you're fit and healthy."

Angelica was examined by the
vet first. "Ow! Your hands are
cold!" she yowled, as the vet
picked her up. She seemed to
have forgotten that she was
supposed to be on her best
behaviour. She moaned and
mewed all the way through the
examination.

Lucinda wasn't much better. Pip
was horrified to see that the
Persian even tried to nip the vet

when he looked inside her ears.

"Here you are," the vet said, looking relieved as he handed Lucinda back to Mrs Walker. "They're fine. And who's this?"

"This is Pip," John replied. "She's sixteen weeks old."

"So she's just old enough to take part in the show," the vet said, with a smile.

Pip wanted John to be proud of her, so she stayed quiet and still while the vet examined her. She couldn't understand why Angelica and Lucinda had made so much fuss. The examination didn't hurt a bit.

"What a sweet kitten," the vet said, as he handed Pip back to John.

"Huh!" Angelica stuck her nose in the air. "Who cares what a silly old vet thinks?"

"Yes, it's the judges you have to impress!" Lucinda mewed, glaring at Pip.

"Now we have to check the cats in and get their entry tags," Mrs Walker told John, leading the way over to another table.

Mrs Walker told the woman sitting at the desk that her cats were entered in the Persian and the Burmese classes. Lucinda and Angelica sat in their baskets, preening themselves, and making rude remarks about the other cats passing by with their owners.

"That Persian's nose is far too pointed," hissed Lucinda.

"Yes," agreed Angelica. "And just *look* at that Burmese over there – her ears are *far* too close together!"

Pip thought that *all* the cats looked very smart. But she didn't make a sound. She was wondering which class John would enter her for. *I hope there is a class for* Kitten with Pinkest

Nose *or* Kitten Coat with Most Colours, Pip thought anxiously. Then at least she might stand a chance of winning a prize.

"I'm John Walker," John told the woman behind the desk. "This is Pip . . ."

Pip pricked up her ears, her eyes open wide.

"And I'm entering her in the *Best Household Pet* class," John added.

Chapter Five

Pip's amber eyes lit up. *Best Household Pet*? Well, she *was* John's pet. And she *did* live in a house. Maybe she had a chance after all!

Meanwhile, Lucinda and Angelica were looking disgusted.

"Look at all those cats!"

Angelica hissed at Pip. "As if *you're* going to be the *Best Household Pet* out of all of them!"

"Yes, don't go getting any silly ideas!" Lucinda spat crossly.

"You'd better take Pip over to the judging area, and get her settled in, John," Mrs Walker said. "I'll see you two later – and good luck, Pip!"

"You'll need it!" Angelica and Lucinda miaowed loudly, as Mrs Walker carried them away.

Pip was very quiet as John took her over to the *Best Household Pet* area. Maybe Lucinda and Angelica were right after all. Maybe Pip *was* going to make a fool of herself . . .

"Look, Pip, I'm going to put you

into this cage here." John lifted up the basket and showed Pip the roomy cage that was waiting for her.

Pip's cage was in the middle of a long row. Most of the other cages already had a cat in them. There was a black cat in the one next to Pip, and a marmalade-coloured cat on the other side. Each cage had a litter tray, a water bowl and a food bowl.

"But first, I've got a few things to get ready," said John. He put Pip's basket down on the floor, and started taking things out of his rucksack.

Pip couldn't see what he was doing, and she didn't much care. She was too busy worrying about what was going to happen when the judging started. What if the judge laughed at her, like Lucinda and Angelica had done? What if he said Pip was too ordinary to take part in the cat show?

"Look, Pip!" John lifted the cat basket up again. "What do you think? Do you like it?"

Pip could hardly believe her eyes. Her cage looked as if it was ready for a princess! John had hung some green velvet at the back of the cage, and he'd put a green velvet cushion with gold tassels inside for Pip to sit on.

"It's beautiful!" Pip purred, rubbing her head against her owner's cheek as he lifted her out of the basket, and placed her inside the cage.

"There's just one more thing." John took Pip's entry tag and slid it onto a narrow piece of yellow ribbon. Then he tied it round Pip's neck. "Now you're all set," he said.

Pip felt she might burst with happiness. So what if she didn't win first prize? John had done all this especially for her. Pip decided that whatever happened, she'd do her very, very best.

"I've got to go now, Pip," John said. "The judge will be coming along in a minute, and the owners aren't allowed to stay while the judging is taking place. Good luck!"

As John gave her a quick pat

and walked away, Pip began to feel scared again.

The judge, a short, round man with glasses, was beginning to make his way down the row of cages. He peered inside each one, then lifted the cat out to look at it more closely.

"Feeling nervous?"

Pip jumped, and turned round. The black cat in the cage next door was purring kindly at her.

"A bit," Pip admitted, as the judge got closer.

"Don't worry," the other cat miaowed. "The judges are always really nice. Is this your first show?"

"Yes," Pip mewed back. "But Lucinda and Angelica, the cats I live with, have been to shows before. They're always going on about it."

The black cat cocked her head to one side. "It sounds like you don't like them very much."

Pip hung her head. "They're not very friendly . . . They're pedigrees, so they're a bit stuck-up," she explained.

"Not all pedigree cats are like that," the black cat replied. "My owner's got a Siamese as well, and we're great mates!"

Pip's eyes widened in surprise. But before she could reply, a shadow fell over her cage. She looked up and saw the judge peering down at her.

Pip's heart beat fast. She felt

very shy.

"Hello, Pip," said the judge, reading the kitten's name from her tag.

Pip didn't think she could even manage a squeak, let alone a purr.

The judge smiled down at her, and gently picked her up. "Let's have a look at you, then," he said, stroking her head.

Looking up at the judge's kind face, Pip suddenly forgot her fears. Angelica's and Lucinda's words popped into her mind . . .

"The judge likes you to lie still, and not struggle or scratch or bite . . ."

Pip didn't *want* to scratch this nice, friendly man.

"The judge wants you to look interested . . ."

Pip *was* interested. She even made a playful grab at the pen peeping out of the judge's pocket. That made him smile.

"Purr a lot . . ."

Pip was purring without even trying. She was really enjoying herself!

In fact, Pip was enjoying herself so much, she felt quite

disappointed when the judge put her down, wrote on his clipboard and moved on to the next cage.

"Well, *that* wasn't so bad!" Pip mewed happily to herself.

The judging took a long time, but Pip wasn't bored at all. There was so much going on around her to look at. And there were the cats next to her to chat to.

But after a while, Pip saw the judge coming back. He stopped by her cage, and stuck a round, frilly shape on the door.

"What's that?" Pip thought, and gave it a sniff. Then she touched the two blue ribbons hanging down from it. It couldn't be anything very important.

Could it?

Chapter Six

"Pip!"

John was running towards Pip's cage. Lots of people were clapping.

"Pip, you've won first prize!" John shouted. "Oh, Pip, I'm so proud of you!"

"What?" Pip mewed faintly.

She'd won first prize? She was the *Best Household Pet*? Pip could hardly believe it.

"Well done, Pip!" John lifted the kitten out of the cage, and hugged her.

"Yes, well done, Pip," miaowed all the cats in the cages nearby.

"Are you the owner of this lovely little kitten, young man?" The judge came up to John and Pip, still carrying his clipboard. "Congratulations. Pip really deserved to win."

"Thank you," John said proudly.

"Like a lot of kittens, she's very pretty," the judge went on. "But what makes Pip special is that she is so friendly." Smiling, he held his pen out towards Pip.

Pip made another grab for it. She liked the judge – he wanted to play too!

"A lot of cats don't really like being handled by strangers," the judge went on. "But Pip makes friends very quickly. I'm sure she'll win lots more prizes in the future!"

Pip felt very proud as John took the frilly blue thing and stuck it on the front of her basket. John told her it was called a "rosette", and the big number 1 on the front showed that Pip had won first prize.

Just then, Mrs Walker rushed over, carrying Lucinda and Angelica in their baskets.

Pip had almost forgotten that the other cats were competing too. There were no rosettes stuck on the front of *their* baskets.

"Oh, well done, Pip!" Mrs Walker exclaimed, when she spotted the rosette. "Aren't you a clever girl!"

Lucinda's blue eyes opened wide. "Pip won first prize!" she howled at Angelica.

"No!" Angelica yowled crossly. "I don't believe it!"

"Did Angelica or Lucinda win anything?" John asked.

The two cats' tails and ears drooped miserably as Mrs Walker shook her head.

In the car on the way home,

Lucinda and Angelica were very quiet.

Even though they hadn't been very nice to her, Pip couldn't help feeling sorry for them. They'd tried their very best to win – and Pip had hardly tried at all. "All those things you told me really helped," she mewed kindly, as Mrs Walker opened their baskets in the living room. "If it wasn't for you, I wouldn't have known what to do!"

Angelica and Lucinda stared at Pip.

"Really?" miaowed Lucinda.

"Yes, really," Pip purred, giving Angelica a gentle nudge with her nose. "So you can *both* share my prize!"

"Oh!" Angelica jumped to her feet. "Well, maybe I can have the rosette pinned to *my* basket for a while!"

"No, me first!" Lucinda hissed, swishing her tail eagerly.

Pip stared at them. "No, I think *I'll* keep the rosette – at least, for today!"

Lucinda and Angelica looked a bit embarrassed.

"OK, Pip," mewed Lucinda.

"Of course, Pip. You won it, after all," Angelica agreed.

Pip purred happily to herself as she jumped onto John's lap later that evening. Lucinda and Angelica were curled up together on the floor, fast asleep. They had been *very* nice to her all afternoon. Pip had a feeling that living with Lucinda Snowqueen Whitepaws and Angelica Spring Blossom was going to be a lot more fun from now on!